Monkey Mischief

Written by
Jill Atkins

Illustrated by
Alex Patrick

Monkey was an orphan.

Amara's father had rescued him from the forest when he was an infant.

Now he had spent his whole life with Amara's family in their house.

Monkey got up to such mischief! He could cheer Amara up if she was ever sad.

One morning, he took a key and ran away with it.

"Come here!" Amara called, but she had to chase him to get it back.

Later that day, Monkey drew with Amara's pencils.

It spoiled her picture, but Amara just laughed.

Then one afternoon, Monkey climbed up inside the chimney.

It was a perfect place to hide, but it was rather dirty and dark.

Monkey peered down at the sheer drop and began to feel frightened.

He could not get down! He wished Amara would come and find him.

After a long time, Monkey could hear Amara shouting for him. Then she appeared below and peered up at him.

"What are you doing up the chimney?" she called, sounding quite severe. "Come down at once!"

But Monkey could not budge. He was shivering with fright.

Amara tried to climb up the chimney, but it was too narrow. So she went away.

From inside the chimney, Monkey could hear Amara shouting to her father.

He was cutting the grass in the valley. Monkey knew from what he said that he would not come to help.

There was a rustling sound, as if someone was climbing onto the thatched roof.

When Monkey looked up, he saw Amara peering down the chimney.

Then a thick rope dropped down to him. He grabbed the rope at once.

So Monkey sat in the dark, waiting for Amara to rescue him.

At last, Monkey could hear Amara's footsteps along the path. He could hear the clip clop of the donkey too.

Then Amara yelled to the donkey. Monkey could hear a clip clop, then the rope tightened.

Monkey held on tight and, inch by inch, he was lifted up the chimney.

At last, he popped out at the top. He was very sooty, but Amara hugged him.

Monkey peered down from the roof. He could see the donkey in the yard. The rope was tied to his collar.

The donkey had rescued Monkey from the chimney!

Monkey held on tight as Amara slid down the thatch.

Amara fetched a tin bath from the barn. Monkey shuddered. He didn't like having a bath.

"Perhaps you won't get up to so much mischief from now on," laughed Amara.

Monkey ran off. He needed to find a better place to hide!